VICIOUSLY BITTEN

USA TODAY BESTSELLING AUTHOR

LEXI C. FOSS

Viciously Bitten

Copyright © 2020 Lexi C. Foss

Editing by: Outthink Editing, LLC

Proofreading by: Katie Schmahl

Cover Design: Covers by Julie

Published by: Ninja Newt Publishing, LLC

Print Edition

ISBN: 978-1-954183-73-5

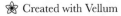 Created with Vellum

VICIOUSLY BITTEN

A Side of Bitten

ABOUT VICIOUSLY BITTEN
A SIDE OF BITTEN SHORT STORY

Sometimes the voices in my head force me to write extra scenes that just don't fit anywhere within the book. That was the case with Damien and several of his moments with Tracey.

The threesome between him, Tracey, and Jace, was too hot to keep to myself. So I put a fancy cover on it and decided to share it with you all.

Just be advised that this hot tidbit features Jace before meeting his heroine, so if seeing him with someone other than Calina will bother you, I recommend skipping the bonus scene.

Happy Reading <3

Once upon a time, humankind ruled the world while lycans and vampires lived in secret.

This is no longer that time.

Welcome to the future where the superior bloodlines make the rules.

Proceed at your own risk.

THE BLOOD ALLIANCE

International law supersedes all national governance and will be maintained by the Blood Alliance—a global council of equal parts lycan and vampire.

All resources are to be distributed evenly between lycan and vampire, including territory and blood. Societal standing and wealth, however, will be at the discretion of the individual packs and houses.

To kill, harm, or provoke a superior being is punishable by immediate death. All disputes must be presented to the Blood Alliance for final judgment.

Sexual relationships between lycans and vampires are strictly prohibited. However, business partnerships, where fruitful and appropriate, are permitted.

Humans are hereby classified as property and do not carry any legal rights. Each will be tagged through a sorting system based on merit, intelligence, bloodline, ability, and beauty.

Prioritization to be established at birth and finalized on Blood Day.

Twelve mortals per year will be selected to compete for immortal blood status at the discretion of the Blood Alliance. From this twelve, two will be bitten by immortality. The others will die. To create a lycan or vampire outside of this process is unlawful and punishable by immediate death.

All other laws are at the discretion of the packs and royals but must not defy the Blood Alliance.

A Note From

Damien

This is not a love story.

This is about sex.

No, not even that.

It's about *fucking*. Harsh, hot, violent fucking.

There's blood. There's biting. There's a hell of a lot of moaning. Some screaming, too.

I'm not an easy lover, but I am a thorough one.

This is meant to be just a taste, a brief glimpse into the darkness of my mind. There's a reason Ryder chose me as a progeny. I'm more like him than anyone may realize. Yet I have my own proclivities as well.

Welcome to my world, loves.

I hope you enjoy this hot little bite.

And if you do, maybe you can convince the master of the pen to write more. Just don't ask for a relationship. That's not in my repertoire.

Chapter One

Tracey

Just knock, I told myself. *Lift your hand. Form it into a fist. Tap it against the door.*

Damien had said to report any and all issues to him. But what if he didn't consider this a problem? He was a vampire, not a human. He might not feel that this qualified as a concern.

I frowned. *This is a bad idea. I should—*

The door opened, revealing a tall, gorgeous vampire with icy blue eyes.

"Do you require something, little human?" he asked, his accent different from Damien's. Crisper, somehow. Hypnotic. His bone structure was flawless, like most of his kind. Although, Damien had a rougher edge, more wicked. This vampire seemed almost regal in stature.

He arched a dark brow at me. "Do you intend to stand there and stare all night?" He looked over his shoulder. "Do most of your staff break decorum in this manner?"

My eyes widened at the question, his reminder of my place causing me to stammer out an apology as I fell to the ground in a bow deserving of his superiority.

"Please, Sire. I apologize. I was… I have no excuse." Because there were none I could give for such a devastating mistake. What had I been thinking? Oh, that was precisely the problem. I hadn't been thinking at all. Would he whip me like Meghan had? Beat me? Drain me? Feast on my organs?

Damien's sigh came from inside the office, the cadence of his boots against the wood floor a familiar caress to my senses. I'd spent the last few weeks in his company, learning his every move and desire. He hated it when I bowed, but surely he would understand the importance now. I'd just disrespected his guest—an unforgivable offense.

"Back up," he said to the other male. "Tracey's a bit timid. We're still working on her training, aren't we, little mouse?" He crouched in front of me, his fingers running through my hair in that soothing way of his. "Look at me, sweetheart."

The words were mildly spoken with a hint of a demand.

We'd been through this routine countless times over the last few weeks. If I didn't obey, he'd force me to look at him. Never cruelly, just by grasping my chin and urging my gaze upward. Damien valued eye contact, which went against all of my training.

Yet I found my head tilting backward now with slightly more ease than before, a part of me eager for an excuse to study his golden-brown irises. There was something dangerously addictive about his features, the harsher edges and masculine lines an enchantment that followed me into my dreams.

While an intelligent part of me understood that I should fear Damien, a very naïve, feminine part of me didn't fear him at all. It had something to do with his blood. He'd lost some of his severity the night he helped me heal after my whipping. Not only had he fed me his essence—an experience in itself—but he'd also held me afterward.

His palm cupped my jaw now, his irises grinning in approval at my obedience. "Good girl," he praised. "Now stand up and tell me what you need."

That final word sent a shiver down my spine. It sounded like a promise from his lips—a promise underlined in a taunt.

I did as he requested, rising to my feet while concentrating on only him. If I pretended the other vampire with the icy gaze didn't exist, I could focus.

Clearing my throat, I quietly said, "Seven hurt her ankle."

He frowned. "Who's Seven?"

"One of the servers downstairs," I explained. Our identities were defined by numbers, and they changed as others died. The oldest member of the staff was named *One*. I'd been *Three* until Damien renamed me Tracey a few weeks ago.

"I see," he replied. "And how did she hurt her ankle?"

I bit my lip, uncertain if I should say. But then that dark eyebrow of his lifted, telling me he would be severely displeased with me if I didn't provide a full answer. "She says she fell," I told him softly. "But I don't believe it's the truth."

"You think one of her superiors hurt her."

"Yes," I admitted, wincing. Had I said the right thing? Would he be angry with the accusation? Should I have said anything at all?

He glanced at the other vampire. "Excuse me for a moment."

"Of course."

Damien refocused on me. "Take me to Seven."

I blinked, startled by his response.

Stop thinking and move, I scolded myself. *Now.*

I spun on my heel and led the way. Damien had tasked me with reporting back any and all injuries to him, which I'd done. What he did with the information wasn't up to me. I just hoped Seven didn't lie to him like she did to me.

Damien didn't appreciate half-truths. I'd found that out early on when he'd asked if I was in pain after being whipped by Mistress Meghan. I'd claimed to be fine. That hadn't been the answer he'd desired. After a very stern discussion, he'd told me never to lie to him again. I'd obeyed him since, answering every question truthfully, even ones that embarrassed me.

Such as his inquiry into how I felt about walking in on him with one of the harem members.

"What did you think of what you saw?" he'd asked me.

It had taken me several seconds to formulate a reply, but I'd recalled his demand for honesty and so I'd provided it. "I didn't understand at first. I thought you were killing her."

He'd laughed. "Hardly." His golden-brown irises had taken on a heated gleam then as he studied me. "How did you feel once you realized the truth?"

"Hot," I'd admitted on a whisper, my cheeks flaming now as I remembered the incident.

Damien enjoyed making his females scream. It had frightened me before I realized they were not cries of agony but of pleasure.

He never made me feel such things because I wasn't part of his harem. I actually wasn't sure what classification I fell into. The servant class, obviously.

However, he treated me more like an assistant than a servant.

He had me arrange his blood-spiked coffee every night, then spent an hour reviewing his schedule with me before providing me with menial tasks to do around his office before releasing me to find him a snack.

"You're thoughtfully quiet," Damien said as we entered the elevator. "Is it Jace?"

"Jace?" I repeated, confused.

"Yes, the royal from my office."

My lips parted. "Th-that...?" *Oh, Goddess...* "I stared at a royal?" It came out as a squeak.

He frowned at me. "You didn't realize who he was?"

"Humans are not meant to look at their superiors," I breathed. "I've never... seen a royal."

"You've seen Ryder."

I shook my head. "No." I never looked upon Ryder. My eyes only ever reached his neck.

Damien sighed. "I'm starting to understand his distaste with society's rules." Rather than elaborate, he pressed his palm to the middle of my lower back and escorted me out of the elevator as we reached the first floor. "Where to?"

My limbs shook as I guided him toward the kitchens, my mind reeling from the reveal of whom I'd boldly stared at in his office.

I'm lucky to be alive, I thought, shocked that Damien hadn't allowed Jace to drain me on the spot. *What is with these vampires and their lax rules?*

Ryder seemed to go against the norm as well, his behavior starkly different from Silvano's. I'd expected Ryder to request my heart the night he'd arrived, as most royals considered such a thing a delicacy.

Then he'd murdered half the vampires in the room instead.

With Damien's help.

I'd stood shocked and mortified, then Meghan had whipped me for displeasing him. Because clearly it'd been my fault—*my unworthy organs,* according to her—that had inspired his rage.

"Little mouse," Damien murmured, his lips dangerously close to my ear. "Your pulse is singing."

I shivered from his nearness, his touch a brand through my blouse. "Sorry, Sire." But I couldn't halt my body's reaction. *I looked at a royal.*

Damien's palm moved to my hip as he spun me around to walk me into the wall beside the staff entrance to the kitchens. We were just off the reception area, tucked into a corridor that only servants used.

"Calm down, Tracey," Damien said, his opposite hand

going to my throat, his thumb nudging up my chin to force my eyes to meet his. "Jace wasn't upset."

I swallowed. "I shouldn't have looked at him."

"Mmm, but I'm kind of glad you did," he replied, his thigh sliding between mine.

"You are?" I whispered, confused.

"I am." His thumb drifted along my jaw, his grip slipping to the side of my neck. "Take me to Seven. Then I'll tell you why I'm glad."

The dark promise in his words made my heart skip a beat. Did I want to know why? I... I wasn't sure. Maybe yes? With Damien, it could mean anything. And whatever I guessed would absolutely be wrong.

Just nod.

Do what he asks.

Stop staring.

But he has such pretty eyes... Actually, his whole face was quite handsome. He had a little scar above his mouth, and I found I rather liked that slight imperfection. It gave him character.

He had more scars on his arm.

Well, not scars. Ink. Black ink.

I'd seen it that day I found him with his harem member. It'd reminded me of black veins, only they covered his left arm in hypnotic little swirls. I couldn't see them now, his dress shirt covering most of his skin. Except at his throat where the top button was undone to reveal some of his pale skin.

I want to lick him there, I thought, eyeing the exposed skin. He had such a fine neck. All corded muscle. Strong. It fit the rest of him, including his dark, messy hair. It fell a bit into his eyes as he watched me, the unruly strands tickling the tops of his shoulders at the sides. Sometimes he tied it back. But not today. My fingers itched to touch his locks, to see if they were as soft as they looked.

"Tracey." His lips quirked up on one side. "Focus, little mouse. Take me to Seven."

I shook my head, clearing it. "Sorry, Sire."

"Never apologize for admiring me," he replied, releasing me. "I'll give you more to admire later."

More? I repeated to myself. *What does he mean by "more"?*

I pondered that as I resumed our path to the kitchen, my mind still whirring without an answer by the time we reached the other servants. They all immediately fell into a bow upon seeing Damien.

He looked them over with interest. Then I pointed to the blonde female struggling to hold her position. "Seven." The girl's head popped up, her eyes widening upon finding herself the subject of his visit. A hint of betrayal flourished in her bright blue eyes as she looked at me, then she immediately forced herself back into a position of submission.

"Everyone except Seven is excused," Damien announced. "But someone inform Chandra that I'm here and I want to see her."

A chorus of "Yes, Sire" met his command.

While he wasn't the royal of this region, his status superseded the others' in this building. I didn't truly understand his role but gathered it to be on the same level as a sovereign. He might even be one. With Ryder being new to the territory, the hierarchy was still unclear.

Damien walked up to Seven and bent to pick her up by the waist. She squealed in surprise, her hands going to his arms before dropping away as though the contact had burned.

I understood the reaction because I'd done the same thing when he'd picked me up from Ryder's floor a few weeks ago. He hushed her just like he'd done me, telling her to quiet as he set her on the counter. That part varied from my experience—he'd carried me back to his room and put me in his bed, not on a marble slab.

"Shh. I'm not going to hurt you," he told her, another similarity to how he'd treated me. Only there was a touch of impatience in his tone now that hadn't existed when we met.

Seven's blue eyes captured mine, pain shooting through her irises. *How could you?* she was asking.

I just shook my head. There was no explaining what I'd done. She wouldn't believe me even if I tried. So I just allowed Damien to lead, his actions far more valuable than words.

His palm ran down her naked leg. As a servant in the kitchens, she wasn't permitted to wear clothes. Every inch of her skin was meant to be bare in case a vampire craved a snack.

Damien had provided me with a skirt and blouse combination, stating he didn't want anyone to confuse my new role with my old one. Whatever my new role meant. Technically, Meghan had given me a similar uniform that night she sent me to service Ryder the first time. But it had come with the expectation of the outfit being temporary. However, Damien's wardrobe requirements appeared to be permanent. At least for now.

I still wore nothing beneath the fabric, but the opaque material hid my natural tones. It'd been strange for the first few days, as I'd gotten used to living without clothing. Sometimes the layers suffocated me, such as now while I watched Damien touch the female with his strong hands.

Why doesn't he do that to me? I wondered, noting the almost reverent way he stroked her calf. When he reached her ankle, she winced. "What happened?" he demanded.

"I fell, Sire," she said. "But I can still work, I swear. Please allow me to prove my worth, Sire. I won't fail you."

He snorted. "You can't work on a broken ankle."

"I can, Sire," she insisted. "Please, I—" She cried out as he did something to her ankle, causing him to grunt.

"You're hurt and can't work," he snapped, releasing her as Chandra walked in. "What happened to Seven?"

"How the hell should I know? She's clumsy and will be turned into food."

"Clumsy," Damien repeated. "How many servants are under your temporary employ?"

"Thirty-nine," the vampire replied.

"And they are all numbered based on how long they've survived, correct?" Damien pressed.

"Yes, which means her time was coming anyway."

"I see," Damien replied, turning away from Seven and wandering to another part of the kitchen. "So when a servant is injured, we turn the worker into food."

"Correct," the thin vampire said, glancing at me. "Or other toys." Her beady black eyes ran over me with interest, leaving me cold.

Damien returned with a butcher's knife, causing my lips to part. I looked at Seven, an apology screaming through my mind. When I'd gone to him, I hadn't expected him to kill her. But, of course, I should have known. She was a defective human. They were slaughtered, not saved.

Except… My brow furrowed. *Except, he saved me. Why?*

"There's a problem with humans in this region, Chandra," Damien said, approaching Seven. "They're dying at accelerated rates, which is creating a food source issue." He pressed the flat of the blade against Seven's arm, drawing it gently down her shaking bicep. She was trying not to cry, her lower lip snagged between her teeth as she fought not to beg for her life.

Because that was what we were taught—to remain silent even in death.

"It's vampires like you who are the problem," Damien continued softly. "I'll inform Ryder that your employment didn't work out."

"What—"

The knife sliced through the air, landing with a crunch in the vampire's head. My jaw unhinged, a gasp escaping me before I could pull it back.

A slow clap started from behind me, the air chilling as the hypnotic voice from earlier said, "Well, that's one way to manage the problem."

Damien lifted a shoulder as he walked over to the unconscious vampire. "It's an effective method."

"One that will infuriate Lilith," Jace pointed out, the heat of his body blanketing my back as he approached me from behind. "That's not to say I disapprove."

"I imagine you wouldn't be standing here if you disagreed with the technique," Damien said as he bent to take the knife out of the vampire's skull. "Do you mind offering Seven some blood? Yours will cure her faster."

"Is that how you intend to save the humans in this region? By offering them all vampire blood?" The royal sounded amused.

"Only the ones I'd like to see live," Damien replied.

Then he walked out the door, leaving me alone with Seven and the royal. I stood absolutely still, my back on fire from his too-close presence.

"Your thundering pulse is an alluring invitation, little one," he whispered against my ear. "But don't worry. I won't touch you without your master's approval."

He slowly stepped around me, his dress shirt brushing my arm along the way, until he stood in front of me. My heart skipped a beat as he brought his exposed wrist to his incredibly perfect lips, his teeth sinking into the creamy flesh to draw blood.

Both of his sleeves were rolled to the elbows, exposing his strong forearms. It gave him a casual appearance that didn't match the underlying intensity in him now.

Why is this so erotic? I wondered, shivering.

That was when I realized I'd held his gaze while he'd bitten his wrist, his silver-blue irises a hypnotic pull that refused to release me.

Look away, I told myself.

Only, I couldn't.

Instead, I chose to drown in the mesmerizing depths of his gaze, oddly unafraid of the death awaiting me at the end.

This was so wrong.

Forbidden.

And burning me up inside.

The fire intensified as he brought his wrist to Seven's mouth, demanding she drink.

What is he doing to me? I couldn't move or think, my feet glued to the ground as a dangerous rhythm started in my chest.

Time seemed to evolve at an unknown rate.

Maybe it stood still.

I felt frozen, yet hot, my thighs shaking with an undefined need.

He has me under his spell, I thought, lost to him. I'd heard about this—the intoxicating presence of a vampire—but I'd never truly experienced it. Not like this.

"Ah, I see why you came down now," Damien mused, returning behind me. "And here I thought it was my strange errand that had piqued your interest enough to follow."

"It did," Jace replied, his eyes still holding mine. "And the pretty little human who delivered the message."

Damien chuckled, his arm circling my waist as he pulled me back against him. "Want to see a trick?"

"Always." He pulled his wrist away from Seven, her groan of disappointment making him tsk. "You've had enough." The way he said it, with such utter dominance, had my thighs clenching with a foreign need for friction.

I understood what it meant. *Desire*. I'd been trained to

11

anticipate it during my coursework at the university. But nothing could have prepared me for the full-blown effect.

Damien nibbled my neck, his strength a solid presence at my back that had me leaning into him on instinct. He made me feel protected. Cherished. Unique.

And I craved all of that right now, the familiarity of his touch anchoring me once more.

"How do you feel right now, Tracey?" Damien asked against my ear. "Hot?"

"Yes," I whispered. "And lost."

"Lost?" he repeated. "In what way?"

"I shouldn't be looking at him, but I can't stop."

"Why not?"

"Because I don't want to," I admitted. "Because he's bewitched me."

Jace chuckled. "I'm accused of that often."

"Enthralling women?"

"And men," Jace replied, his eyes grinning at me. "Was the trick her honesty?"

"Yes," Damien murmured, his lips grazing my neck. "She's always truthful, even when it breaks her conditioning."

"Which is why she came to you about her friend."

"I told her to inform me of any injuries or untoward behavior." Damien released me to walk over to Chandra again. I didn't understand his intention until a glint of silver caught the lighting overhead, followed by a thud that broke me from Jace's intrusive stare.

A shudder worked through me as the vampire's dark head rolled across the floor. Jace was there in the next moment, his woodsy scent enveloping me and distracting me from the gruesome scene. Still, he didn't touch me, but I felt utterly consumed by his presence.

Ryder possessed a similar appeal, his age and superiority a

cape that engulfed the entire room when he entered it. At least, that was how it'd felt the first night he arrived.

Jace's charisma was different, less intrusive yet equally dominant. His regal air provided a false sense of safety. It struck me as dangerous because I knew better than to trust him, but I could feel myself wanting to fall into his arms and accept his guidance.

He boasted the kind of aura that could seduce a woman into following him directly to hell, to be tortured and maimed, all while smiling with gratitude for being chosen as his victim.

It both frightened and excited me.

"Do you want to play with her?" Damien asked, walking over to stand beside Jace and face me.

"Depends," Jace murmured. "Are you offering me Seven or your little mouse?"

"Seven exclusively," Damien replied. "Or…" He trailed off to brush my hair over my shoulder, exposing my neck. "You could help me introduce Tracey to the finer parts of vampire life."

"She hasn't indulged in a taste yet?" Jace asked.

"Not with me," Damien murmured. "Have you ever been with a vampire or a lycan, Tracey? Sexually, I mean."

Goose bumps pebbled down my arms, my throat working hard to swallow. "N-no, Sire. I've not been bitten, either." There had been several close scenarios throughout my short time as a restaurant servant, but I'd managed to survive them unscathed.

"I imagine she went through training at the university," Jace said. "Right, little human?"

"Y-yes, My Prince," I breathed, recalling my courses.

"Did any of them include two men at once?" he asked.

Oh, Goddess… "No," I managed to say, my voice barely audible. Two vampires at once would kill me, surely. Had I disappointed Damien? Was this meant to be a punishment?

They both stood before me, their domineering auras nearly bringing me to my knees.

I wasn't sure if I should beg for my life… or something else entirely.

Jace studied me for a long moment, some of his amusement leaving his expression. "She's scared."

"Which is precisely why she needs the introduction," Damien replied, reaching for me. "She's timid, but trainable. And she deserves a reward for doing exactly as I asked, despite it frightening her. I'd say that proves her strength and ability to handle it."

"It'll be a challenge," Jace murmured.

"An enjoyable one," Damien agreed, glancing at him. "If you're up for it."

Jace's silver-blue eyes left mine to take in the other male. "Do you think you can handle sharing your mouse? I don't want to end up with a black eye."

"It would be temporary," Damien replied. "The black eye, I mean."

"And the sharing."

"Yes, I suppose that, too."

Jace nodded. "Then I'm game, so long as your little mouse is agreeable."

"That may require some convincing," Damien replied, refocusing on me. "Why don't you escort Tracey up to the penthouse while I clean up down here?"

My heart hammered in my chest at Jace's answering expression. "Providing me with the first taste?"

Damien smiled. "I think she needs the appetizer. But don't you dare move on to the first course without me."

"Of course," Jace agreed. Then his hypnotic gaze captured mine again. "Come on, little one. Let's get better acquainted upstairs."

Chapter Two

Jace

TRACEY TREMBLED BESIDE ME, her growing apprehension an aphrodisiac to my vampiric senses. Every shaky exhale taunted the predator within me, demanding I cage her in and go for a bite.

Soon, I promised, pressing my palm to her lower back to guide her into the elevator, where she entered the code for Damien's suite. Ryder had given him the penthouse, a fact that I'd found interesting when we'd first arrived.

However, Tracey's knowing the codes to that floor was even more fascinating. It signified trust, something I doubted Damien bestowed on just anyone. I wondered if she realized that.

"He likes you," I said softly. "Which is why we need to set some ground rules." Because I hadn't been joking about the black eye.

While I wouldn't mind a little roughhousing, I feared a negative outcome should the two of us engage in such an affair. If Damien chose to become territorial in the middle of our dalliance, it wouldn't end well for either of us. That was the downside to playing in groups, particularly with two vampires who favored alpha tendencies.

I might be older than Damien, but I sensed his strength. He was a force of nature I didn't want to disturb.

"Rules?" Tracey repeated, a slight tremor in her voice.

"Yes, rules," I murmured. "To ensure safety."

Her big brown eyes blinked up at me before immediately glancing away. My lips twitched. She thought I meant to "bewitch" her. It was true that vampires possessed certain abilities to compel; however, I hadn't used it on her at all. I'd merely held her gaze to see if she had the strength to maintain my stare, which she did.

The elevator dinged, announcing our arrival. I applied pressure to her lower back, urging her to enter the suite. It took up the entire floor, something I already knew since Damien had allowed me to take over one of the guest rooms. It'd been a respectful move on his part, a way of acknowledging my superiority in ranking.

As a royal, I could command use of the suite and harem, not that I would. But he'd offered it readily, then took me to his office to begin reviewing the analytics for this region. We'd only gone through a few hours of data before I sensed the human lurking outside his study door.

Tracey, I mused. *Damien's little mouse.*

It was an apt description, as her head barely cleared my shoulders, and she had a slender waist. But her tits were nicely sized, the blouse unbuttoned just enough to reveal a hint of creamy cleavage.

She was braless, something I could see by the stiff outline of her nipples through the white fabric. And the hint of her growing arousal in the air suggested she wore nothing beneath her skirt as well.

Damien was quite clever, providing her with clothes that hid her assets while ensuring just enough of her remained on display to tease.

"How long have you worked for Damien?" I asked, leading her toward the bedroom I'd been given for the next few days.

"I was assigned to Silvano Region after the last Blood Day," she said softly.

When she didn't elaborate, I looked at her. "That's not what I asked. How long have you been with Damien?"

She glanced at me again, her shoulders rigid. This conversation didn't appear to be helping to loosen her up. "We met a little over two weeks ago." It came out so soft I almost didn't catch it all.

My instincts fired, informing me there was more to this than she was saying. "How did you meet?" I opened the door to the bedroom but paused on the threshold. I blocked her way with my shoulder against the doorjamb, needing this answer from her first.

She refused to meet my gaze, her focus on my shirt. "The night Ryder arrived, I did not please him appropriately, so I was whipped. Damien helped me heal."

My eyebrows hit my hairline. "Ryder whipped you?"

Her brown eyes jumped up to mine. "No. Mistress Meghan did."

"Mistress Meghan?" I repeated. "Who the fuck is Mistress Meghan? And why would she whip you for not pleasing Ryder?"

Tracey cleared her throat, her gaze leaving mine once more for the riveting buttons on my shirt. I caught her chin and forced her to look at me.

"Explain," I demanded, out of patience for this submissive routine. While it served an enlightening purpose in the bedroom, it was most infuriating when trying to hold a normal conversation.

"She used to manage the restaurant. Damien killed her, like he did Chandra tonight."

"Why?"

She shook her head. "I don't know. He stated that Mistress

Meghan was mismanaging the staff. He didn't provide an explanation for Chandra."

"Did Ryder ask for you to be whipped?"

"I don't know," she said slowly, frowning. "I don't think so. He was very angry about it and had his harem favorite help clean up my back."

The "harem favorite" must have been Willow.

"Then Master Damien arrived and brought me up here and gave me his blood to help me heal," she finished.

"I see." That explained why he hadn't touched her yet. He'd been giving her time to acclimate. "What have you done for him these last two weeks?"

"I help around his office," she said. "I ensure he's fed."

"But not with your blood," I mused, fascinated by the tidbit she'd revealed earlier about not being bitten.

Her cheeks turned a pretty pink. "No. He hasn't requested my blood."

"Something tells me he will tonight," I informed her, pushing away from the doorjamb and taking a step backward into my room. "I know I will."

She visibly swallowed, her heartbeat an intoxicating cadence that expressed her hesitation and excitement. I adored this moment with humans—that precious indecision where they didn't know whether to run or to get down on their knees and beg.

"Come here, Tracey," I said, beckoning her forward with my tone. "Don't worry. We still have the rules to discuss." I kicked off my shoes near my overnight bag, then sat on the bed.

She entered without closing the door, her steps uncertain as she moved to stand in front of me. I held out a hand for her. She eyed it warily before accepting, and I gently pulled her between my legs, then set her hand on my thigh.

The positioning was purposeful, as it granted her a slightly superior edge by allowing her to look down at me rather than up. Although, her shorter height lessened the angle, but it was enough to provide her with at least a semblance of control.

"Breathe, Tracey." I kept my voice soft, coaxing. "We're not going to do anything to you that you won't enjoy." I doubted she believed me, but there wasn't much I could do beyond promising not to harm her and later proving it to her through action. "Which sexual courses did you take at the university?"

Her throat worked again, her pulse a thundering invitation against my ears. "Oral studies with male and female, an advanced deep-throating course, and one penetration class."

"Vaginal or anal?"

"Vaginal."

I nodded. "All right." That meant double penetration was probably off the table for tonight. It would be too much for her to handle, and if she experienced pain, it would set Damien off.

Protective energy had wafted off of him the moment she'd arrived. Knowing that he'd provided her with his blood to aid in healing, yet didn't feel the need to do the same for Seven downstairs, also spoke volumes.

He cared about Tracey.

I didn't want to provoke an untoward reaction by harming a female he seemed to consider his—even if he hadn't admitted that fact to himself.

So I needed to tread carefully.

Her current swaying told me I also needed to do more coaxing before we truly began.

I reached for hips, holding her steady between my sprawled thighs. "Was there anything in your studies that you didn't enjoy? And don't lie to me." It exhausted me when a human claimed to be okay with all things sex, only to express displeasure during the eventual act. While the university demanded they accept all activities, I did not. If the human despised the activity, it truly soured the moment for me.

She remained quiet for so long that I wondered if she intended to ignore the question. Then finally she admitted, "Female oral is not my preference."

"What about receiving oral?" I asked her.

Her flush crept down into her neck. "I don't mind receiving."

"You don't mind having your pussy licked?" I repeated, chuckling. "Well, we'll have to fix that outlook. You should love it. But what about sucking cock? Is that something you 'don't mind' as well?"

Her pretty blush had to be touching her breasts by now. It was interesting how some humans could have this conversation without batting an eye, and others, like Tracey, exuded exquisite embarrassment at the topic. It told me she wasn't very well versed in the sexual arts. I typically preferred my females to be more experienced, but I'd make an exception tonight.

"I received decent scores in deep-throating," she informed me matter-of-factly.

"That doesn't tell me if you enjoy it or not, Tracey."

Her pupils flared. "I enjoy things I'm skilled at."

I arched a brow. "And do you feel you're skilled at deep-throating cock?"

"I am," she confirmed, her confidence at odds with her demure behavior of moments ago. Perhaps she felt challenged by my tone. Well, if that were the case, we'd play on that a bit.

"I look forward to you proving that to me, little one." I drew my thumbs along her hip bone, considering our next steps.

While her self-assured response was a move in the right direction, I still sensed her hesitancy and concern.

"Hmm." I studied her, my gaze dropping to her pert tits. "I think we should start by removing your clothes."

Rather than do it for her, I released her and leaned back on the bed, propping myself up on my elbows.

"Undress." I didn't phrase it as a request but as a demand. Mostly because I wanted to see what she'd do.

Her fingers visibly shook as she lifted them to her blouse to slowly pop open each button. Goose bumps pebbled down her sternum, her flush indeed touching the tips of her breasts. Little rosebud nipples stiffened to eager peaks as she dropped the shirt to the floor. Then she moved on to her skirt, a snap and a short zip later revealing I'd been right before about her lack of underwear. Her bare cunt made my mouth water, the hint of glistening flesh between her thighs a beacon to my male senses.

She bent to remove her shoes last, the heels strapped around her slender ankles. "Stop," I said, sitting up. "Place your foot here." I gestured to my thigh.

Tracey shivered but did as I requested, her balance impressive.

"Grab my shoulders if you feel as though you're going to fall," I said, not wanting to risk her harming an ankle like Seven had downstairs.

I ran my fingers over her calf, down to her delicate ankle, then deftly unbuckled the black strap. She released a shaky exhale as I gently pulled the shoe off.

"Are you sore?" I asked her, running my thumb along the instep of her dainty foot.

Her flinch answered my question before her nod. "Only a little."

"Were you standing a lot today?"

"I'm not used to heels," she admitted softly. "Or clothes."

"Because your servant position required you to remain nude," I translated, nodding. Releasing her foot, I requested the opposite one and removed the heel. Then I slid back on the bed, making room for her to join me. "Climb up here and lie beside me. We're going to work on your opinion of oral sex."

"And what opinion is that?" Damien asked, appearing in the doorway.

"She doesn't mind receiving it," I informed him.

Tracey's pulse escalated, her breathing pattern changing to a more erratic rhythm. Both reactions were tells in favor of Damien's presence, her attraction to him evident in the way her nipples beaded even more in response to his nearness. He obviously knew how she felt, hence his suggestion we share.

He entered and closed the door behind him, then leaned back against it with his hands tucked into his slacks. "Then it seems I arrived just in time to observe the appetizer."

My lips curled. "Observe?"

"You're much older and more experienced. Perhaps you'll teach me something."

"I'm certain I could," I admitted before refocusing on Tracey. "Why are you not beside me on the bed? I'm not a fan of repeating orders."

Her heartbeat jumped upward another notch. "I'm sorry, My Prince," she said.

"Don't apologize. Move," I ordered.

She visibly trembled, her gaze wandering back to Damien briefly before she crawled onto the bed. Her tits swayed as she moved toward me, her eyes on the comforter the whole way. Then she went to her back beside me, her head barely on the pillow.

I eyed her stiff form, then shot a look at Damien. He appeared amused. "My women tend to look a little more comfortable," he told me conversationally.

"Mine, too," I admitted. "Your timid mouse seems to think I'm going to eat her."

"Well, aren't you?"

I smirked, then looked down at Tracey, her brown eyes

blown wide with a mix of arousal and concern. "Yeah, I am," I told him, holding her gaze. "I'm going to devour every inch of her."

"Good," Damien replied. "Because she smells delectable."

I bent to inhale the aroma of her thrumming pulse. The alluring invitation, coupled with the aroused fragrance coming from between her thighs, had me growling in approval.

"Try to relax, little one," I said against her ear. "It'll make this so much better for you."

Chapter Three

Tracey

Try to relax? A royal vampire just said he intended to *devour* me. And Damien had approved of his intentions. How the hell was I supposed to relax?

"Shh," Jace whispered, his lips a caress against my neck. "Let me take care of you."

Take care of me? I repeated to myself. Was that another way of describing my impending death?

My fingers curled into fists at my sides, my heart hammering violently in my chest. I closed my eyes, praying to the Goddess that he made this quick.

And then I felt his tongue trailing downward to my breasts, tasting my skin, searching for a place to bite. My lungs stopped working as he captured my nipple between his teeth, my mind fracturing into a plea to beg him not to hurt me there. I'd seen it done before, had overheard the agony of having that body part ripped off from vicious vampire fangs.

A tear rolled down my cheek, my innate terror overriding the hum of approval growing between my legs.

Vampires could make their victims love the sensations, even while they died.

I didn't want that.

I preferred to go with dignity.

"Tracey."

Please don't, I thought. *Please don't make me like it. Please.*

"Tracey."

My fists tightened even more, my legs tensing for the blow, the inevitable pain, the harsh bite of vampire fangs.

It'll all be over soon, I promised myself. *There are worse ways to die.*

"*Tracey.*" The rumble in Damien's tone made me flinch, my eyes squinting open to find him standing beside the bed and staring down at me.

I frowned, confused. Jace was no longer touching me. In fact, he wasn't even next to me, but standing on the other side of the bed. I hadn't felt him leave.

"Breathe," Damien coached, his caramel-brown eyes swirling with intent.

I inhaled on impulse, my body his to command. Then I exhaled and inhaled again, my lungs oddly tight as though I'd forgotten how to use them.

"Good girl," he praised. "Keep going."

I watched his chest, my own breaths mimicking his, until my heart began to slow to a more functional pace. He reached out to cup my cheek, his thumb tracing my lower lip.

"Jace isn't going to hurt you," he said softly. "I won't let him."

I started to glance toward the royal, but Damien held my face captive with his palm.

"Tracey," he said, going to his knees beside the bed and leaning forward to bring us to eye level. "Do you remember what you saw the other day? When you walked in on me in the bedroom with Monika?"

Monika, I thought, annoyed by the name. She was one of the harem girls. And I very much remembered walking in on him with her. "Yes."

"You thought I was killing her, but later realized I wasn't hurting her at all," he reminded me. "Jace wants to make you scream in pleasure, not pain. Just like I did with Monika."

"Why?" I whispered.

"Well, I think because you provided a dissatisfactory response to a question about oral sex," he said, glancing at the other male.

"Among other reasons," Jace replied, his deep voice a sensual caress that sent a strange sort of tingle down my spine.

Damien chuckled. "Yes, among other reasons. Such as the fact that you're a beautiful woman whom we want to share." He drew his thumb across my lower lip again. "Let us show you what it can be like, sweet mouse. I promise you'll like it and crave more."

My heart fluttered as he leaned down to press a kiss to my mouth, his caramel-brown eyes swirling with dark promise. He gently nibbled my lip, then skimmed his nose along mine.

"Spread your thighs for Jace," he whispered, his cinnamon scent surrounding me in a fog of hypnotic bliss. "Let him taste you."

I swallowed, my legs slowly parting beneath his command.

"Good girl," he praised, his palm sliding to the back of my neck. "Now focus on me."

"I am," I told him, lost to his gaze.

Then I felt hot hair touch my ankle just before Jace's mouth met my skin. I jolted at the contact, my skin pebbling with gooseflesh.

"Shh," Damien hushed, his lips returning to mine. His tongue slipped inside to soothingly stroke mine, his unexpected kindness distracting me from the male below.

What are they doing? I wondered, feeling lost and hot and flustered all at the same time. This wasn't what I'd been trained to anticipate. They were being *gentle*—an adjective I'd never assign a vampire.

Damien's mouth coaxed mine into responding, his kiss an

enchantment that overtook my mind. I returned the embrace on instinct, my tongue dying to mate with his.

Mmm, and speaking of tongues, Jace was using his to draw a path along my inner thigh. A dark thought struck me—something about the femoral artery—but the graze of Damien's teeth demanded I entirely concentrate on him and his mouth.

I moaned as a warm wave of sensation slid over me, heating every inch of my exposed skin. Damien's kiss enchanted me, his touch a possession against the back of my neck. He ran his thumb over my pulse just as Jace's tongue met my intimate flesh.

I gasped, my back bowing up off the bed in response to that initial stroke. Then he latched onto my clit, causing my eyes to fly open. I hadn't even realized I'd closed them.

Damien stared down at me, his irises seeking a response I didn't know how to give.

My lips parted on a protest, only for a groan to slip between them instead.

Ohhh...

The warmth inside me turned into a brewing fire, sending zips of electricity through my veins that left me convulsing against the bed.

This was nothing like my university experience.

Jace applied just enough pressure, his mouth a caress I didn't know I needed until he provided it. Energy flowed from his fingertips as he skimmed my thighs, his prowess rampant and alive from that slight touch. My legs parted wider to accommodate him, my body begging for more, which he gave by slipping a finger inside me. Then two.

"There she is," Damien murmured, approval evident in his tone.

I gazed up at him, confused, and cried out as Jace sucked my sensitive bud into his mouth.

It was too much.

Yet too right.

I wasn't sure if I should protest or thank him. Mmm, definitely the latter. Oh, yes, *absolutely… Ohh…* My mind stopped working, the eruption below a hot spike to my senses that blackened my vision and sent spasms through my limbs. The climax happened so suddenly, so immediately, that I almost didn't understand what it was. That had *never* happened during my class exams. Not like that, anyway. This was a shattering underlined in an intensity I didn't know how to define.

All because of Jace's mouth and clever hand.

And Damien's kiss.

How? Why? Oh, Goddess, I hope he keeps doing that…

Jace's tongue massaged me in a manner that seemed to prolong the pleasure, creating a new whirlpool of sensation to blossom inside me. It almost hurt in its severity, yet I couldn't stop shaking in response.

Part of me wanted to tell him to stop.

But that part wasn't in charge now.

No, a wanton side of me desired to feel that again, just so much more.

Damien grinned, a hint of dimples flashing at the edges. "Now we can properly begin," he said softly.

I frowned at him. *Begin? Haven't we already started?* My mouth didn't work enough for me to voice the questions, my throat dry from the lust darkening his eyes to a deeper brown.

He lowered his lips to my breasts, his tongue licking a path right to my nipple. Fear spiked inside me, only to be dulled by the rapture of him sealing his mouth around my tight bud.

Another hot wave caressed my skin, shooting me toward an ecstasy I knew existed. Not a climax, not yet, just utter oblivion of having two mouths feasting on my flesh as if I were the most cherished delicacy in the world.

They didn't bite.

They only nibbled.

And sucked.

And licked.

And introduced me to a new meaning of life.

I threaded my fingers through Damien's thick hair, no longer caring about rules or propriety. He'd correct me if I overstepped any boundaries. The royal between my legs growled in approval, his fingers hooking upward to massage a point inside that had me seeing stars.

My lips parted on a scream I couldn't hold back, the world exploding around me in a cataclysm of *heat*. Words left my mouth that I didn't understand, a flurry of praise mingled with fear and an urging for them to stop, yet it was the last thing I wanted. It was just so much. Too much.

Nothing should feel this good.

Am I dying? I wondered, light-headed and seeing spots. I nearly laughed. If this was death, then I welcomed it.

A light prick between my thighs shot me up out of my thoughts, drawing my gaze downward to a pair of icy blue eyes. "How do you feel about receiving oral sex now?" he asked against my throbbing clit.

I moaned, trying to twist away from him, but his hands on my hips held me in place. Damien had stood up again, his expression amused as he looked down at me. "Answer the royal," he demanded.

I shivered, the reminder of Jace's title making my blood thrum faster in my veins. "I…" I trailed off, thinking through my response. Damien valued honesty, so I knew better than to lie. "That wasn't like my training."

"In a good way?" Jace pressed. "Or do you still feel oral sex is inadequate?"

"Phrased a different way, would you like more, little mouse?" Damien asked.

My cheeks heated at the question. "Right now?"

"Right now," he replied.

I squirmed a little, uncertain. "I feel like I'm on fire."

"That's how you should feel," Damien murmured. "So do you want more?"

More pleasure? To feel as though I were floating and high on life? "Yes." But I also wanted something else. Something darker. Forbidden. A need I couldn't exactly articulate other than to say, "I want to taste you." I didn't direct it at one particular person, as I meant the phrase for them both.

Who am I? I marveled, feeling oddly bold, like somehow they'd gifted me a sliver of control through the act of worshiping me.

Or maybe it was just trust.

They hadn't hurt me; they'd pleased me. And while it might be temporary, I could easily find myself craving more, desiring another round of intensity even at the expense of a little pain.

"You want to taste us, little mouse?" Damien mused, his golden-brown irises grinning. "I think that can be arranged." His pupils dilated, his inner predator peeking out as he began unbuttoning his shirt.

My mouth watered at the sight of all that toned, hard masculinity beneath the fabric. His core boasted a strength that made me feel small in comparison, his muscles rippling with each move. And then he revealed those sexy arms, the ink along his left limb making my mouth salivate with the need to lick him.

"She looks famished," Jace murmured.

"She does," Damien agreed. "I think you should feed her your cock while I devour her cunt." His shirt fell to the floor as he kicked off his shoes.

Jace shifted toward the bottom of the bed, his fingers—still glistening from my arousal—went to the buttons of his shirt to follow suit. Then the mattress dipped beside me as Damien lay down.

"Come straddle my face, beautiful," he said. "I want you to drench me in your sweet scent."

"Peaches," Jace mused, his hand falling to his belt. "That's what she reminds me of."

"My favorite," Damien drawled. "Get over here, little mouse. Now."

I swallowed, my heart thudding in my chest. It took considerable effort to lift myself up off the bed, my body slower and softer than usual. But one look at Damien spurred me on, his hungry gaze holding a dominant edge I couldn't ignore. I started to move over him, only to be instructed to switch directions to face away from the headboard.

"Use me for balance if you need to," he instructed.

It wasn't a position I'd ever done before, and it made me feel oddly vulnerable as I pressed my knees into the pillow on either side of his head. Then his palm came up to my ass, forcing me downward. My hands landed on the bed alongside his hips, my face close to his groin, only to have a hand guide my chin upward.

"We're going to work on your multitasking abilities," Jace said, his pants unzipped to reveal his black boxers beneath. They barely contained his erection, the thick shaft a pulsing promise of the *multitasking* he'd just mentioned.

Damien's teeth skimmed my folds at the same time, causing me to hiss out a breath. He wasn't as gentle as Jace, his touch rougher and filled with a purpose he underlined as he nibbled my clit. *Is he going to—*

My arms gave out on me as his teeth sank into my flesh, his bite throwing me into an orgasmic spiral with no hope of surviving. It consumed me, destroyed my ability to think and breathe, and left me panting against his groin.

"Well, I'm glad my cock wasn't in your mouth just then,"

Jace drawled, his fingers combing through my hair while I trembled uncontrollably from Damien's bite.

That's what it feels like? I marveled. *Dear Goddess, that's… that's… ohhh…*

Damien started licking me again, his mouth hungry and hot against my core. I couldn't stop spasming, the pleasure shredding every ounce of thought I could potentially conceive. Until a tug against my scalp had me looking up at the royal beside the bed.

"Did you forget your task, little one?" He'd lowered his pants and boxers to reveal his thick arousal. It was perfectly proportioned to the rest of him, a study in pure masculinity and grace. His touch slid from my hair to my chin as he guided me upward and toward him. "Open that pretty mouth for me."

I felt compelled, as though his very words forced my body to cooperate, yet deep down I knew I was obeying all on my own.

Because I wanted to taste him.

To feel him.

To prove my worth after the exquisite pleasure he released into my system.

All the while, Damien remained between my legs, his mouth an enchantment against my damp flesh.

I should be passed out from the pleasure by now, yet his hum brought me back to life with a vengeance and pushed me into a new horizon of existence.

My body knew how to handle this.

My mouth knew exactly what to do.

I allowed my instincts to drive me, my lips parting around Jace's soft skin to glide down his shaft as deep as my throat would allow. He groaned in response, his silver-blue eyes glimmering with approval and a hint of surprise.

He hadn't expected me to do that.

And for whatever reason, that had me wanting to do it

again. To shock him with my ability, to prove to him that I knew what I was doing despite my earlier misgivings.

Damien's bite had chased away my doubt, his grip on my hips reassuring as he slid his tongue along my sex. Each lick whispered an unspoken vow for more, the rapture resolute and palpable.

He wanted me to understand what it meant to be cherished by him. He wanted me to experience the bliss of a vampire's touch. He wanted me to forget my concerns and merely *be*.

So I did all of that and more, letting my experience and teachings reign as I sucked Jace with a skill I'd always been afraid to use.

Until now.

Tonight.

With them.

His fingers knotted in my hair, urging me onward, his abs flexing with each thrust into my mouth. He'd only placed one knee on the bed, his foot still on the ground, angling me slightly away from Damien and into the position Jace desired.

My nails dug into the comforter as I held myself upright. Then Jace told me to grab his hips. I followed his command because I wanted to touch him. However, it came with the added benefit of lessening the strain on my back.

Damien growled in approval as I gave him more of my weight, sitting fully on his mouth as I maintained my grip and balance using Jace's hips.

An erotic dance began between us, provoked by Jace's groans and Damien's tongue. I lost myself to the sensations, taking Jace deep into my mouth and moaning against his shaft as Damien grazed my clit with his fangs. This time I was prepared for his bite, but that didn't make it any less potent.

Jace's cock absorbed my cries of pleasure, his grasp in my hair keeping me where he wanted me as he drove deep into my throat. It was beautiful chaos. Oblivion. Unreal. *Insanity*.

I cut off my mind, forcing myself just to feel and take it. To allow these men to play with me as they saw fit. To simply exist in a sea of ecstasy and rely on them to keep me afloat.

Jace's icy blue eyes pierced mine, holding me captive as he plunged into my mouth. He had the body of a god, his muscles rippling and creating an intoxicating view from my position at his groin. I could stare at him like this all day.

"Use your tongue," he instructed me. "Yeah, like that."

I picked up on his signals, followed his requests, took him deep, and swallowed around his head. He groaned in response, the tendons in his neck tightening. I learned what he liked, repeating the action, then varying my tongue, and starting all over again.

He cursed. "That's it, Tracey. Do that again."

I did, and his resulting groan made my thighs clench. Damien nipped me in reply, causing me to yelp. He chuckled against me. "Time to switch positions."

Jace pulled out of my mouth. "Up," he said sharply. I didn't understand until Damien lifted me off of him and rolled off the bed.

I sat back on my heels, uncertain of where they wanted me.

Then Damien started taking off his pants, and my ability to comprehend anything went right out the window.

Jace was all tall, lean muscular lines, while Damien had a bit more build to him. His shoulders were wider but tapered down into a waist comparable to Jace's. He stood a little shorter than him, yet still several inches taller than me.

And both men were endowed in a similar sense, with Jace being longer and Damien being fuller.

They were stunning displays of masculinity and strength, making me feel small in comparison. "How was her mouth?" Damien asked.

"Adequate," Jace replied.

"Just adequate?"

"She was a little distracted," Jace murmured.

"So her multitasking could use improvement."

"Yes, but the potential is absolutely there."

Damien nodded. "Then let's work on it more. Mouth or pussy?"

"She's your little mouse," Jace said, his eyes on me while he spoke. "You choose."

"I want her cunt," Damien murmured. "Besides, I want to know if her mouth lives up to expectations in the end."

Jace smiled. "Likewise."

They both started toward me, their intentions clear. This time my heart raced in anticipation, not fear. And from the hungry gleams in their gazes, they could hear it, too.

"Come here, little mouse," Damien said, his voice deep and powerful as his knee met the mattress. "Let's play."

Chapter Four

Damien

TRACEY HAD COME undone in the most beautiful manner, just as I'd predicted. I knew a seductive feline existed beneath the meek exterior. I just had to coax her out of hiding. And she stared at me now with a come-hither gleam that made me want to fuck her right into the damn bed.

The taste of her on my tongue had been a flavor unlike any other, the reward of her compliance one I cherished more than I anticipated. Something about her spoke to me on a level I didn't quite understand yet.

It started the night we met, when I'd witnessed the furious female beneath the broken exterior. She'd hated relying on others to help her, not that she'd admit it out loud. However, I'd seen the defiance in her gaze as she drank from me—a prideful spirit wounded by the need to rely on another.

Most in her position would have eagerly accepted my essence, taken more than their fill, and hoped for more afterward. But not her. Instead, she'd spent the better part of the last two weeks trying to help me in any way I demanded.

My own little mouse, scurrying around to do my bidding.

But she didn't scurry now.

No, she went up onto her hands and knees to crawl toward me, her tits swaying along the way. I changed my mind in an instant, that mouth of hers too sinful to ignore. Threading my fingers through her hair, I pulled her to me. "Open" was the only warning I gave before guiding her downward and parting her lips with my cock.

"*Fuck*," I breathed, hitting the back of her throat without any resistance on her part. "That's better than adequate."

"You have her undivided attention," Jace murmured, sliding onto the bed to draw his finger down her spine. Tracey jolted beneath his touch, but her mouth remained beautifully engaged, her groan a vibration I felt all the way to my balls.

Jace drew his touch lower, over her ass, to the damp place between her thighs.

She cried out from whatever he did—I assumed he slid his fingers inside, but couldn't see from my angle—and I tightened my grip in her hair. "Learn to endure it," I told her. "Focus."

Jace chuckled as he apparently took that as a challenge to see how far he could push her. I didn't mind, because each moan reverberated against my shaft, which proved to be a desirable sensation.

I kept one foot braced on the ground, my knee on the bed, as Jace went to his knees behind her. His gaze met mine, a question lurking in his depths. I suspected he didn't typically ask for permission to fuck a woman but was choosing to respect my preference here because he saw Tracey as mine. I didn't bother to correct him, mostly because I supposed she did belong to me.

Dipping my chin, I gave him the approval he sought and held Tracey's mouth to me as he lined himself up with her pussy and drove his hips forward.

Her shock came out as a cry that soon melted into a moan.

He didn't go easy on her, his grip brutal on her hips, but my little hellcat took it like a queen. Her eyes glazed over with the sweet lust I preferred to see on a woman's face, her cheeks a bright pink of passionate exertion.

I drew my knuckles across her flushed skin, then traced her

jawline with my thumb. "You look so beautiful like this," I praised her. My opposite hand remained in her hair to help guide my movements into her mouth while Jace took her harshly from behind. One of his hands slid beneath her, eliciting a guttural groan from her in response.

"I think she likes that," I said.

"She's not the only one," Jace replied, quickening his pace. "She's fucking tight."

"Mmm," I hummed, gazing into her eyes. "How do you feel, Tracey? Is this the taste you wanted?"

Her nostrils flared, that feline inside her pacing behind her eyes.

I smiled. "I think she wants more."

"She's never done anal," Jace informed me, confirming they'd spoken about her limits before they began. That didn't surprise me. He struck me as the kind of male who takes care of his lovers, even those he considered temporary—like Tracey.

Gliding my thumb along her jaw, I considered that information and murmured, "Yet."

She swallowed around the head of my cock then, making me groan out a curse. Because *fuck*, that felt good. "Again," I demanded.

She skimmed the underside of my shaft with her teeth instead, causing me to arch a brow. "Is that a threat, kitten?" I asked her, the upgraded nickname seeming appropriate for the moment. Because my little mouse had just grown claws.

Her throat worked around me, but not before grazing my sensitive skin once more with her blunt teeth.

I slid out of her mouth and bent to capture her lips with my own, punishing her with my tongue. Using my grip on her hair, I yanked her upward, forcing her to grab my shoulder for balance while Jace remained inside her from behind. It bent her a little, but her flexibility had proven admirable before, so I took advantage of it now. She panted against me, Jace's thrusts brutal and demanding. Her eyes glistened with tears, the arch in her back driving him deeper and right up into her precious spot. "Come for him," I demanded, noting the flare of her pupils. "Squeeze the life out of his dick with that pretty little pussy and *come hard*."

I sank my teeth into her lower lip, flooding her veins with the endorphins I knew would drive her over the edge and carry him with her. Her cry of pleasure was underlined in pain, her upper body giving out against me. I caught her with ease, holding her through the agony and licking the wound I'd created on her plump lip.

"*Fuck*," Jace grunted, pistoning into her. "So fucking good." His head fell back on a groan, his hips slamming into hers as he released himself inside her.

I'd been with a few men but preferred women. However, there was something undeniably captivating about watching a male like Jace fuck. Power rolled off him in waves, intoxicating me and drawing me into the moment.

The second he pulled out of Tracey, I took his place behind her, plunging inside her without warning while he cradled her head and kissed the hell out of her. She was in that same arched position between us, only more so now because he knelt completely on the bed. It allowed her to pillow her breasts against his chest, which was almost as hot as watching his tongue dominate hers.

She was no longer coherent, her body having fully given in to the authority of our beasts. It painted a beautiful picture, her submission and trust gifts for us to accept and cherish as we unleashed the full power of our affection on her.

Jace drank from the wound I'd created while I pounded into her, her sheath a perfect fit for my cock. "You like that, don't you?" Jace asked her, his tongue tracing her lip. "He's making you feel so good."

Tracey whimpered, her response unintelligible.

"You're going to come one more time for us," he informed her softly, almost reverently. "Then we'll give you a break before doing it all over again."

Her sound of protest made me smile and fuck her harder, then I leaned into her neck to bite her again. She screamed, the pleasure too much for her mortal form. Jace was right there with the antidote, the scent of his royal blood driving me onward as he captured her mouth to feed her his essence. She shook from the onslaught, her petite form absorbing the brunt of my strength and brutality.

A growl ripped from my throat as she clamped down around my shaft, her orgasm ripping the pleasure straight from my balls and throwing me into a dark oblivion underlined in *need*.

More, I thought, the word on repeat in my mind as I continued to fuck her through my pleasure. *Fuck, I need more.*

However, I felt her body weakening, the experience too much for her. I caught her around the waist, holding her as the last of my seed emptied into her. Jace had her face as well, his palm gentle against her cheek. He smirked as she fell into blissful unconsciousness between us.

"Was that what you had in mind for an introduction?" he asked me, his blue eyes glittering.

"Only if you agree that we're doing that all over again as soon as she wakes up," I replied, shuddering from the aftershocks of my orgasm.

"Absolutely," he agreed. "She still needs a lesson on anal."

"And double penetration," I mused.

"How long did you intend to give Ryder with his pretty little hybrid? A week?"

I nodded in confirmation, easing away from Tracey to help Jace rearrange her on the bed. Her dark hair sprawled out against the white pillows, her lips parted on a sigh. I swiped my thumb across her bottom lip, gathering the blood there and bringing it to my tongue. Jace's essence had mingled with hers, providing a decadent flavor that had my cock twitching in preparedness.

The royal noticed, because he smirked. "I have that effect on others."

"Blood is power," I replied.

"Indeed it is." He brushed Tracey's hair back away from her face, his expression thoughtful. "She's rather resilient for a little mouse."

"Yes." I pulled blankets out from beneath her to properly tuck her in, then lay on the bed beside her while Jace stretched out along her opposite side. "She's more like a kitten."

"I'm a fan of claws."

My lips twitched. "Is that why you go for lycans?"

"It's one of the many reasons I indulge them, yes," he murmured, releasing her hair and drawing his touch downward to her breasts. I pulled on the sheet to expose them for him and grinned as her nipples beaded beneath his touch.

"She's learning already," he mused, leaning forward to capture the bud between his teeth. She mumbled something unintelligible, her eyes remaining closed. He blew against her wet skin, stirring an array of goose bumps to rise across her breasts. "A week should be enough for a reasonable introduction."

"We'll need to work on her stamina," I pointed out, chuckling as she muttered a protest and squeezed her thighs together.

"And her ability to multitask," he returned. "Although, she admittedly improved during our session."

"We'll see how she does during the next one."

"Yes," he agreed softly, returning his head to the pillow beside hers. "Wake me when she's ready."

I curled myself around her, pulling her hips into mine. The moment she stirred, my cock would tell me. "Will do."

Then I closed my eyes, breathing in her sweet scent mingled with Jace's woodsy appeal. Not a bad way to end an otherwise long night.

I cupped her sex, noting the fluids marking her flesh.

She'd be sore when she woke.

But soon she'd grow used to taking cock.

Particularly, mine.

While Jace might prefer lycans, I enjoyed wildcats. And something told me Tracey would turn into the wildest of all. She just needed a little nudge.

I kissed the back of her neck, my hand remaining between her thighs.

"Sleep well, kitten," I whispered into her ear. "We'll play more tomorrow."

I hope you enjoyed this sexy little bite from the Blood Alliance world! I'm not sure what's going to happen with Damien or Tracey yet, but I'm looking forward to exploring their voices more at a later date.

Meanwhile, Jace's story is up next in *Kingly Bitten*. He claims to want a lycan. Calina says otherwise.

Cheers xx

Once upon a time, humankind ruled the world while lycans and vampires lived in secret.
This is no longer that time.

Calina

I have thirty-six hours to live.
Thirty-six hours to find a solution.
Thirty-six hours to kill them all.

My friends. My family. My subjects.

It's a cruel fate, one my maker subjected me to over a century ago when she placed me in this hell. I learned then that freedom is a falsehood. Escape doesn't exist. I'm a ticking time bomb, slated to erupt.

Until *he* appears from above. A vampire. A walking god with icy blue eyes. He claims to be our salvation, but I see him for who he really is—the devil in disguise.

Jace

I don't want to be king, but I'll become one if it means I can have *her*—the gorgeous ice queen I found waiting for me inside Lilith's labs. She feigns indifference, claiming I do nothing for her, but I see the embers stirring in her stunning hazel eyes.

Only there's more to her than a pretty little face.
She's neither vampire nor lycan.
An immortal without a classification.
A secret I must now contain in a world collapsing in chaos.

Welcome to the new beginning.
My name's King Jace. Allow me to be your guide…

Available on Amazon

ABOUT LEXI C. FOSS

USA Today Bestselling Author Lexi C. Foss loves to play in dark worlds, especially the ones that bite. She lives in Atlanta, Georgia, with her husband and their furry children. When not writing, she's busy crossing items off her travel bucket list or chasing eclipses around the globe. She's quirky, consumes way too much coffee, and loves to swim.

Want access to the most up-to-date information for all of Lexi's books? Sign up for her newsletter here.

Lexi also likes to hang out with readers on Facebook in her exclusive readers' group — Join Here.

Where To Find Lexi:
www.LexiCFoss.com

Book Five: Blood Bonds

Book Six: Angel Bonds

Book Seven: Blood Seeker

Mershano Empire Series - Contemporary Romance

Book One: The Prince's Game

Book Two: The Charmer's Gambit

Book Three: The Rebel's Redemption

Midnight Fae Academy - Reverse Harem

Ella's Masquerade

Book One

Book Two

Book Three

Noir Reformatory - Ménage Paranormal Romance

The Beginning

First Offense

Royal Fae Wars - Omegaverse Paranormal

Wicked Games

Underworld Royals Series - Dark Paranormal Romance

Happily Ever Crowned

Happily Ever Bitten

X-Clan Series - Dystopian Paranormal

Andorra Sector

X-Clan: The Experiment

Winter's Arrow

Bariloche Sector

Other Books

Scarlet Mark - Standalone Romantic Suspense

Made in the USA
Monee, IL
26 October 2021